HANK BROOKS

THE HOSTAGE

GAY ROMANCE

WARNING

This book contains sexually explicit scenes and adult language. It may be considered offensive to some readers. This book is for sale to adults ONLY.

* * * * * * * * * * * * * * * * * *

Please store your files wisely where they cannot be accessed by underage readers.

Please feel free to send me an email. Just know that these emails are filtered by my publisher. Good news is always welcome.

Hank Brooks – **hank_brooks@awesomeauthors.org**

About the Publisher

4Fun Publishing, a member of **BLVNP Incorporated**, 340 S. Lemon #6200, Walnut CA 91789, info@blvnp.com / legal@blvnp.com
NOTE: Due to the highly emotional reaction of some people to works of erotic fiction, any email sent to the above address that contains foul language or religious references is automatically deleted by our anti-spam software and will not be seen. All other communications are welcome.

DISCLAIMER

The Hostage

Gay Romance

By: Hank Brooks

© Hank Brooks 2014
ISBN: 978-1-62761-731-4

Part One

They were warned not to go out there.

"The town is full of blood-thirsty insurgents," the captain said. "They hide in civilian homes. They use mothers and babies as human shields. You never know when one of them will snipe at you from behind a woman, or from the other side of a closed door."

But Trevor Lawrence was not to be discouraged. He wanted an interview with an insurgent and he wanted it badly. He wanted the hatred to spew out of one of them in his own words. He especially wanted the bastard to claim that it was the will of Allah. It was his intention to show the world that they were not soldiers of Allah or freedom fighters, as they claimed, but blood-thirsty murderers, hiding behind innocent women and children, and behind God.

He commandeered a Jeep during the night, and he and his Arabic speaking cameraman, Ahmed, set out toward the nearby town just before dawn. The small population of the town was just awakening when Trevor and Ahmed got there. The first life they saw was a young boy sitting aimlessly in a doorway. They stopped, and Ahmed brazenly asked the youngster where the soldiers were. The boy gave out a little sob and waved his head, indicating that they were behind the door he was sitting in front of.

Trevor parked the Jeep, and he and Ahmed approached the door. They knocked. There was no answer, so they opened it anyway. Ahmed entered first, and was instantly shot in the heart. He died without knowing what hit him. Trevor was luckier. He was surrounded and knocked unconscious by two insurgents.

When he awakened, he found himself propped up against a wall. His hands were tied behind him with a heavy rope. The rope was course and was biting into his wrists. His feet were also tied at the ankle with the same rope. Heavy duct tape was covering his mouth. His head felt light and the room seemed to be spinning around him. He was sick to his stomach, and he wanted to vomit, but that would be impossible with his mouth taped shut. He had to control his urge to spew up, or else he could drown in his own puke.

He looked around. He was in a bare room with one small window high up one of the walls. It truly looked like a prison cell. The heat in the room was unbearable. He was alone, and his head was throbbing. He knew instinctively that he had been moved to a different location, probably some insurgent hiding place. He passed out again, just as he became aware that he had to pee.

In his sleep, he felt someone shaking his shoulder. "Wake up, Trevor," he heard a voice commanding him, and he thought, *Thank God. It's all a dream.* The shaking got more insistent, and he realized that he wasn't dreaming at all. He opened his eyes with great difficulty.

A tall, thin man hovered over him. He needed a bath, and he emitted a putrid body odor. He sported a mustache and a small beard, which incongruously was well trimmed, because he could very well do with a haircut. His breath was also a surprise. It was sweet smelling, as if he had just brushed his teeth or eaten a breath mint. He was naked from the waist up. Of course he was. The heat in the room was truly oppressive. Trevor would have liked to have stripped also.

In spite of the situation, Trevor had to admire the man's torso. He was solid and muscular even though he was so thin. Once past his body odor, Trevor also realized that the guy was very handsome indeed. His almost black eyes stared into Trevor's, until Trevor had to turn away.

"What are you doing here? What do you want?" the man asked in perfect English. Trevor was shocked. He had a million questions of his own, and would gladly have answered the man's questions, but his mouth was taped.

Suddenly, his captor roared with laughter. "Forgive me," he said. "I forgot about the tape." That said, he ripped off the tape in one quick movement, leaving Trevor's lips burning with pain.

"Now answer my questions," he said, not unkindly.

"How do you know my name?" Trevor asked.

The man retrieved Trevor's wallet from his pocket and waved it at his captive. "Now answer my questions!"

Trevor lied. "I wanted to interview one of you, so that I could show the world that you men fight for a cause, and you aren't the cold blooded killers most non-Muslims believe you to be."

The man roared with laughter once again. "You expect me to believe that dribble, you Jewish Israeli slime."

"Actually, I'm an American from Fresno, California, and I'm a Christian; Presbyterian to be exact."

"What's the difference? You're all the same. We can't convert you non-believers, so we will have to kill you."

"You're off to a good start. Why did you kill my cameraman, Ahmed? He was a Muslim."

"We could not know that, and we wanted his camera equipment so we could photograph you, and send pictures outside to show what we do to spies."

"I'm not a spy."

"So you say."

"Can I know the name of my friendly captor, and how come he speaks perfect English?" Trevor asked.

The man sat down right next to Trevor and rested his rifle on the floor on his side, away from Trevor.

"Here's the situation, Mac," the man said. Trevor couldn't wait to hear. This guy was as American as he was.

"My name is Martin Spenser. My mother, Janina, is a Saudi. She married an American who worked for one of the big oil companies. After my father's hitch, they moved back to Chicago, his home town. I was born and grew up there. My father did not practice his religion, but my mother secretly instructed me in the teachings of Islam. She taught me to detest the unbelievers and to bring Islam to the world."

"Did she tell you to spread Islam through murder?"

Martin's face clouded over. "It's not murder to do the will of Allah. It's a duty and a privilege."

"Rot in hell," Trevor said, and he turned his head from Martin's. Martin hit him on the head with the butt of his rifle, and Trevor was unconscious once again. When he awoke, he knew immediately that he had been moved once again. He was in a completely different room. Martin could see the confusion on his face.

"We move around a lot so you unclean pigs can't find us so easily. Right now we are in an abandoned cabin in a remote part of the mountains, and we are alone. There is no way you can escape. We have plenty of provisions and water. I am going to untie your hands and let you clean up a bit.

Then we will rehearse a little speech that you will recite for the camera. You are going to tell the world that your captors are very kind to you, considering that you are a spy, and that you are being treated very well."

"You're kidding, aren't you?"

"Do I look like I'm kidding?"

Trevor realized that he hadn't really looked carefully at Martin since he woke up again. Obviously the man had bathed. His body smelled clean and he had groomed himself somewhat. His long hair was neatly combed.

He had shed his dirty clothing, and was wearing only a pair of American style boxers. Trevor could see Martin's black pubic hair through a small gap in the fly of his underwear.

"There are two things that are a must," Trevor informed Martin. "First of all, I need to pee badly, and I am not in the habit of wetting my pants. The second thing is that if I don't get rid of some of this heavy clothing, I'm going to die of a heat stroke, and your propaganda campaign will be over."

"I am a humane man," Martin smiled. "Your wish is my command." He untied Trevor's hands and feet, and immediately Trevor stripped to his boxers.

"I'm glad you're wearing boxers," Martin said. "I think that jockeys are very unattractive for a man, and very slutty." Trevor was very surprised at that last remark. It sounded very gay, and he should know, because he was gay.

"Where can I pee?"

"I'll take you outside, but first I need to retie your hands." Martin retied Trevor's hands behind his back, and led him outside. The first thing Trevor saw was his Jeep standing just outside the cabin. He saw it as a means of a possible escape. All he had to do was get hold of the keys. Since Martin was only wearing boxers, the keys were not on his person. He needed to find out where Martin had put them.

"I've been peeing behind those rocks," Martin said, and they walked behind the rocks. There was no road to be seen anywhere, and Trevor wondered how Martin had maneuvered the Jeep through the desert and the mountains.

When they got behind the rocks, Trevor saw a beautiful mountain stream running just a few feet away. There were also many cypress trees along the banks of the stream. It gave his area of captivity, a kind of serenity.

"How do you expect me to get my cock out of my underwear?" Trevor asked.

Martin just smiled, and he walked behind Trevor. He put his arms around his hostage. To Trevor it felt like a caress. Martin unsnapped the clasp in Trevor's boxers. Then he took out Trevor's rod and aimed it at the rock.

His touch was gentle and feathery and in spite of himself Trevor began to erect, but he didn't get totally hard as he began to pee. When he finished, Martin shook off the excess drops, and wiped the slit dry with his finger. Trevor got stiff again and leaned back into Martin, who continued to stroke Trevor's cock very gently.

Unable to restrain himself, Trevor was able to grab Martin's cock with his bound hands. Martin was as stiff as he was.

"Thank Allah that you are circumcised," Martin said. "I could never touch an unclean, uncircumcised cock."

"It doesn't matter to me if you are cut or uncut. Just don't stop doing what you are doing." But Martin did stop, leaving Trevor with a severe case of blue balls.

"Homosexuals will never see Allah's paradise," Martin said. "I helped you pee, and nothing more."

Trevor was not convinced. He had been with enough men to feel the passion in Martin's touch.

"How will you get the film out of here?" Trevor asked just to change the subject.

"About once a week we'll get a short visit from a courier. He'll replenish our provisions, take the camera with all your recorded messages, and replace it with a new camera."

"Are you telling me that I must continually tell lies which you will record? How long do you intend to keep it up?"

"They will not be lies," Martin spat. "They will be truths that I will script for you. We will keep it up as long as those fools continue to search for you. Do as you are told, and you will not be harmed."

"You will kill me in the end, so why should I *LIE* for you?" Trevor emphasized the word, *lie*, and he could see Martin's eyes narrow into slits.

"I said that I would not harm you if you cooperated."

"Hah! Great! So one of your sick buddies will do the deed."

"Believe what you will, but trust me I can make life very miserable for you or very pleasant. It all depends on your attitude and cooperation."

Trevor did not bother to answer. He knew it was useless. Instead he decided to plan a strategy to let the world know that he was forced to say what he did. He had no idea yet what that would be, but he knew from experience that experts would be studying his facial expressions as he spoke. He also knew that Martin was familiar with his culture so he had to use extreme care.

"I'm hungry," he told Martin. "Make my life pleasant." Martin smiled, and Trevor hated himself for thinking, *what a beautiful smile.*

"Does that mean you'll cooperate?"

"Let's just say I'll think about it. In the meantime, I'd like to know where you bathed. I need a bath badly."

"In that stream a few meters behind these rocks. Come, I'll take you there."

Part Two

The stifling air seemed to cool down at least ten degrees on the shore of the small mountain stream, which was shaded by the cypress trees along its banks. Martin undid the ropes on Trevor's wrists. He sat down on a rock with his rifle aimed at Trevor.

Trevor dipped a toe into the stream and was pleased with the water temperature. He dropped his underwear and waded in.

"Aren't you going to join me?" he asked.

"Not this time. I bathed a short while ago."

Not this time. I guess Martin would join him another time. Trevor hoped so, but again he hated himself for thinking such thoughts. Martin was the enemy and he had no intention of sleeping with the enemy, no matter how attractive.

Trevor washed himself as best he could without soap. Nevertheless the romp in the cool stream was very refreshing and he hated to come out. After he emerged, he realized that he had no towel so he laid himself down on the grass and let the sun dry his body. Martin just sat with his rifle pointed at his hostage. He was strangely quiet.

"Next time can we bring soap and towels?" Trevor asked.

"Of course. I was unprepared to take you here today. Next time will be different."

Trevor could only wonder what he meant by next time. Would Martin join him in the water…naked? He hoped so. When he felt that he was dry enough, Trevor stood up and put on his boxers. Martin stood up also, his rifle still pointed at Trevor.

"We had better get to the cabin and out of the sun soon," Martin said. "The afternoon sun can be brutal." Trevor was pleased that Martin did not put any ropes on his wrists. He reckoned that Martin considered him to be no danger with a rifle constantly pointed in his face. He was afraid the ropes would be reapplied at bedtime.

"I'll make us something to eat," Martin said. "After lunch we will rehearse your first message to your pig friends. I have already written it."

There were two knapsacks lying in the corner of the room, along with both their clothing. Martin removed a slab of cheese from one of the sacks. He broke off two small pieces and he gave one to Trevor. He carefully returned the remaining cheese to the sack. Then he opened the other sack and removed a large, round loaf of bread. Again he broke off two small pieces and offered one to Trevor. Apparently, that was to be the menu for all times, since Trevor could not see any other food around the place. He wondered if the keys to the Jeep were in one of the sacks, or in the pocket of Martin's trousers lying alongside.

After what passed as their lunch, Martin restrained Trevor again. He walked out of the cabin without closing the door. Trevor could see him getting something out of the Jeep. He came back, closed the door, and laid out two sleeping bags on the floor. He made no explanation to Trevor but he reached into the pocket of his trousers and he took out a little piece of paper. Yet again he untied Trevor's wrists and handed him the paper.

Trevor read:

Hello friends. This is Trevor Lawrence. As you know I am a journalist with CNN. My cameraman Ahmed and I invaded insurgent territory on the pretext of wanting to interview some of them. Our real mission was to spy for UN forces. We were captured and we were separated but my captors tell me that Ahmed is alive and well and he is being well treated. As for myself, I am being well fed and treated humanely. This is a pleasant surprise since they know that I am a spy. I think they will want to swap me for one or more of our prisoners at a later date. Time will tell.

"Do I have to lie about Ahmed?" Trevor asked. "It isn't fair to give his family false hope. He has little children."

"It can't be helped. Ahmed was a soldier in the fight for Islam. Someday his children will learn of his martyrdom and be proud. Now read and memorize the message and be sincere. I want you to convince me that you are telling the truth. Remember, I can make your life misery or paradise. It's up to you."

Trevor read the message several times. He pretended to take a long time to commit the message to his memory. He was stalling for time, and still no plan came to him. Finally, as he recited the first word, he conceived a plan.

For no reason at all, he got a picture in his mind of Humphrey Bogart playing Captain Queeg in The Caine Mutiny. When he testified at the court martial, Queeg betrayed his insanity by rubbing steel balls in his hand. Trevor had no steel balls, but he decided that he would hold his hands perfectly still in his lap when he was telling the truth. When he was telling a lie he would begin to rub his fingers together in a slow motion, but when he was telling a whopper, he would rub his fingers in a more agitated manner. If he did this at every taping, he prayed the experts would pick up on it. He could only pray that Martin would be too busy with the camera to notice.

Martin had substituted his rifle for the camera. "When you look in the camera," he instructed Trevor, "pretend it's my rifle and behave yourself. Smile occasionally. If you cooperate, I have a special treat for you for dinner. If you try to fuck it up, you can watch me eating your treat, and you'll get nothing to eat, not even water." Trevor had to take the risk. He recited the message rather convincingly and rubbed the fingers of his right hand together at the appropriate time. He also smiled occasionally, but only when he was lying. He hoped that would be an additional clue to the experts to indicate that he was being forced to recite this bag of lies.

Martin seemed pleased at the result. "See how easy that was?" he asked.

"So what's my treat?" Trevor asked. He knew what he wanted but it wasn't going to happen.

"I've got a cooler in the Jeep and it's full of fresh melons. We'll have some with dinner."

Dinner consisted of a piece of cheese, a smaller piece of bread, and a sliver of melon. After dinner Martin said, "I'm sure you have noticed that we have no electricity. We have about an hour of daylight left. Do you play gin rummy?"

"I haven't played in years. Perhaps you could refresh my memory."

"I used to play with my father," Martin said wistfully. "He taught me." He produced a deck of cards from out of his trousers. Trevor wondered how many other little treasures were in the pockets of the trousers lying neglected on the floor. The keys to the Jeep, he hoped.

They sat facing each other on the floor. Their legs were folded under them, producing a gap in the fly of both their boxers. Trevor could see Martin's dark pubic hair again, and he was sure that Martin could see his blond pubes. They played until it grew too dark to see. Martin put the cards away and started to tie up Trevor.

"Please," Trevor said, "don't do this. Where could I go if I wanted to escape? I have no idea where I am." He was very shocked when Martin relented and threw the ropes on top of his discarded clothing.

"I'm a very light sleeper," Martin warned.

Trevor had hoped that Martin would put the two sleeping bags close together, but alas, he put his bag clear across the other side of the room. Fortunately, it was clear across from the knapsacks and clothing also. It had cooled down considerably once the sun set, and both men crept inside their sleeping bags.

Trevor willed himself to stay awake. He was rewarded when he heard Martin snoring slightly. Quietly, stealthily, he stood up and went over to Martin's trousers. He reached into the right hand pocket because he noted that Martin was right handed. There were the keys he so desperately sought. Clad only in his boxers he crept out of the cabin and sat down behind the wheel of the Jeep. He put the key in the ignition and got only a cranking, groaning sound. He tried again and again, but the Jeep would not start.

"Are you having trouble?" he heard Martin ask.

Martin was standing outside the Jeep holding out his hand. Trevor removed the key, got out of the Jeep and handed the keys to Martin.

"I removed the wires to the ignition," Martin said in a very matter of fact way. He was grinning broadly, almost laughing. "I knew you would try something like that. I would have been disappointed if you hadn't. Just don't try it again. Now, let's get some sleep. I want to tape another message tomorrow."

Trevor was dejected, but he followed Martin meekly into the cabin. He lay down once again and crept into his sleeping bag. He was shocked when Martin brought his bag right up to his, and laid it down so that they were actually touching. "I see I have to keep a sharper eye on you," Martin said. He crept into his bag and mumbled something that sounded to Trevor like 'g'ni.'

In the middle of the night, Trevor awoke. Martin was breathing into his ear and it had disturbed him. The room had been pitch-black when they retired, but now moonlight streamed through a dirty window. Trevor glanced at Martin. He had come out of his sleeping bag and was lying on top of it. He was on his side, and was sort of hunkering up to Trevor. Martin's leg was covering his cock, and Trevor could not get a glimpse of it.

Suddenly, as if in answer to a prayer, Martin rolled over and onto his back. His very hard cock was pointing straight to the ceiling through the fly of his boxers. Trevor gasped. Martin's cock was very fat and at least eight inches. He wondered if it got bigger in the heat of passion. Trevor longed to take that cock into his mouth, or sit on it and take it into his ass, but he didn't dare.

He got out of the sleeping bag, and lay down on top also. He sidled as close to Martin as he could, and he let the back of his palm touch Martin's leg. He was afraid to go further, so he lay like that for a long time unable to breathe. Finally, Martin rolled over in the other direction, and they were no longer touching. Trevor finally fell asleep.

In the morning, they relieved themselves behind the rock. Martin dug a little hole which served as their commode. When they were done, he covered their dung. We'll wash later in the stream," he said. "If you don't cooperate, you can walk around all day with a shitty ass."

Trevor desperately wanted to bathe naked with Martin, and he did indeed behave himself. He taped the next message as convincingly as he could, but he smiled at the biggest lies, and rubbed his fingers together along with his smiles. If Martin was suspicious, he didn't show it.

When the taping was done, Martin led them to the stream, but he didn't stop. He walked a bit farther upstream. "It's deeper here," he explained. "We'll be able to get in almost neck high." They dropped their boxers and Martin laid two towels on top of them. He had a bar of soap in his hand, but it was laundry detergent. Neither of them cared.

They soaped themselves alternately and then Martin handed Trevor the soap and said, "Do my back, please." Trevor was shocked, but very excited. He took the soap and started soaping Martin's neck. Little by little he went farther down Martin's back.

"I haven't felt this clean in weeks," Martin said. "Aaaah."

Trevor was nearly in a trance. He soaped farther and farther down Martin's back. He didn't even realize it when he started to soap Martin's buttocks. Martin made no move to stop him. Trevor began to rub the soap up and down Martin's crack, and without thinking, he inserted a finger in Martin's most private part. Martin sighed and pushed himself farther back against Trevor, forcing Trevor's finger further up his ass.

Suddenly, Martin pulled away, turned around and faced Trevor. His eyes were blazing with anger and he slapped Trevor hard across his face. "Faggot," he yelled. "You won't drag me to hell with you."

The two men glared at each other, Martin with hate, and Trevor with disappointment. Neither said anything. They left the water and began to dry themselves. Trevor was frightened. He was certain that he had overstepped his bounds, and that Martin would see to some severe punishment.

They started back to the cabin. When they entered it, Martin closed the door, grabbed hold of Trevor and began to kiss him with an open mouth. Martin put his lips up against Trevor's ear. "Be very quiet," he said. "We are being observed, and the cabin is most likely bugged."

The cabin remained eerily quiet after that. Trevor was afraid to say anything. He knew that the cabin was probably bugged for sound, but after careful scrutiny, he was sure there were no hidden cameras staring at them. Martin would not have kissed him if there were.

They made small talk when they ate, and also when they played gin rummy. Otherwise, they spoke hardly at all. Finally, it grew too dark to see anything, and they got ready to retire. Martin put both sleeping bags close together, and he lay down on top of his. Trevor heard a slight rustle and figured out that Martin had removed his boxers. He did the same and lay down on top of his bag with his stiff cock throbbing in expectation.

"Don't pull the same crap you pulled last night," Martin warned out loud, and then in an instant he was on top of Trevor, kissing him passionately.

Martin whispered in Trevor's ear, "I will do everything I can to keep you safe, and get you back to your people as quickly as possible, but you must never speak of this. If my comrade's found out about this, we'd both be dead as quick as you could say Martin Spenser." He slid down Trevor's body and took Trevor's hard cock into his mouth. Trevor put his fist in his mouth in anticipation of what was coming. He came quickly, too quickly for both their wishes. Trevor had to bite hard into his fist to keep from emitting any noises. Martin swallowed all that Trevor had to offer.

When Trevor recovered a bit, he returned the favor. Martin had to bite his fist also. Afterward, they held each other tightly, and just before they separated for the night, Martin whispered again. "Tomorrow, in the stream, I think it will be safe to fuck each other in the deep water."

In the water the next day, they pretended to be splashing each other and romping around. They somehow managed to enter each other's asses, but they did not dare start to fuck for fear of discovery. They were able to play like this for the next few days, but at night they went down on each other and came to a mind blowing conclusion. They were frustrated about not being able to cum in their asses, but they had no choice for fear of being discovered.

Every day, Trevor taped a message to the outside world, penned by Martin. Martin did not seem to notice the phony smiles and the fluttery fingers, and Trevor allowed himself to believe he was getting away with it. His only fear was that when the tapes were sent out, the experts would not pick up on his shenanigans.

One morning, Martin was extremely cold to Trevor. "This is the day the courier is coming. I don't know what time he'll get here, so you will have to forgive me for this." He found the ropes he had previously discarded and tied Trevor's hands behind his back. He had Trevor sit on the floor and he tied his ankles together. Trevor said nothing. He just stared forlornly at his captor.

He was shocked when Martin took out a piece of duct tape. Before Martin could tape his mouth, Trevor said, "I have heard that prisoners very often fall in love with their captors." He stared hard at Martin. "I'm no exception." Martin looked like he was about to cry, and he slapped a piece of tape across Trevor's mouth.

The courier did not arrive until mid-afternoon. Trevor was bound the whole time. Martin did not even feed him the entire day. Very few words were exchanged between the courier and Martin. The courier took the camera and gave Martin a new one. It was very inferior to the one stolen from Ahmed. He also brought in a few bags of provisions and exchanged a new cooler for the old one. On his way out, he kicked Trevor in the ribs and spat out one word. "Pig!" Martin winced.

Martin wanted to make sure that the courier would not return unexpectedly. He waited almost two hours, until the sun began to set, before he untied Trevor. As he did, he kept hugging him without saying a word. Both men were crying. When it grew dark and they got ready to retire, they held each other tightly and cried bitterly. They did not make love that night. They just held on to each other as if they were clinging to each other for dear life. They slept that way all night.

They were awakened before dawn by the sound of several vehicles approaching the cabin. Martin put on his boxers, grabbed his rifle and ran to the window. Trevor put on his boxers also, and watched Martin intently, fearing for his life.

"Thank God," he heard Martin say.

The cabin door opened and several US Army personnel entered. It was still dark, but one of them shone a flashlight into the room. Another lit a gas lamp and illuminated the room. The sergeant with the flashlight, turned it off, stood straight, and saluted. He smiled broadly and said, "Lieutenant Spenser, sir. It's good to see you again." Then Martin and the sergeant shook hands. Trevor was struck dumb.

"You don't know how glad I am to see you, Jim. How did it go?"

"According to script, sir. We killed twelve of their top honchos, and a few paeans to boot."

"Great! Now get us out of here. We need a decent bath, a decent bed, and transportation back to the States ASAP." Martin threw Trevor's clothes at him. "Get dressed, Trev. We're out of here."

"What the fuck is going on?"

"I'll explain everything later. You're going to get a good news story for CNN; I promise you."

Part Three

Martin was two weeks shy of graduation from West Point when he had to fly back to Chicago to attend his father's funeral. Martin, Sr. had passed away suddenly from a severe embolism in his brain. Martin stayed with his mother, Janina, for a few days after the funeral, and then they flew back together for his graduation.

While Martin was in Chicago, he and his mother had a visitor. It was Janina's uncle, her father's brother, from Saudi Arabia. They were both shocked to see him because Janina had no contact with her family back home at all, except for one letter she had received from her sister when her father died. Nevertheless, they were cordial and hospitable to the man.

Ibrahim only stayed a couple of hours, but he made it quite clear that Martin's place was as a soldier in Allah's army and not the United States Army. He admonished Martin to honor his dead grandfather. He gave Martin a card, and said, "I know you will do the right thing. Here's where you can reach me when you see an opportunity to serve Allah."

During his stay, Janina was polite and stayed in control of herself but as soon as he left, she began to scream. She was hysterical and Martin had great difficulty calming her down.

"I hate them," she screamed. "If your father hadn't rescued me, I'd be dead."

"What do you mean?" Martin asked. He was appalled. His mother had never spoken of her life back in Saudi Arabia until now.

"They treat women worse than pigs," she started to explain. "Once, my veil accidently slipped from my face. We were out in public and I was only sixteen. I adjusted it quickly, but when we got home, my father beat me until I lost consciousness. 'This is a warning,' he said. 'One more indiscretion like that and I will kill you. You acted like a whore.' I lived in a constant state of fear. I celebrated when I heard of his death through my sister.

"When I was eighteen, I got a clerical job at the oil company where your father worked. We fell desperately in love." She smiled remembering those days. "I mentioned my growing feelings to my father. He said that if I married outside the faith, he would kill me, and it would be considered justifiable by the community. When I told your father how much my father opposed our marriage, we got married secretly, and he spirited me out of the country one day on the company airplane. What gall Ibrahim has to try to recruit you for his murderous plans."

During his growing up years, Janina had instructed Martin in the tenets of her faith, but she never encouraged him to embrace Islam. In fact, she encouraged him to embrace Martin, Sr.'s faith. Unfortunately, Martin, Sr. did not believe in God, so Martin never really felt a part of any religion.

He attended Protestant services at West Point, just because it was mandatory to attend any religious service, and to be one of the boys. However, there was one thing that kept him apart, and would never allow him to be one of the boys.

When he graduated from The Point he was still a virgin. He knew since middle school that he was gay, but he could never act on it. He had no interest in women, and he remained a virgin until he settled in at his first duty station in California. There he became friendly with another graduate from his class.

They knew each other, of course, but had never buddied around at West Point. Here at the base, however, they had a common bond, having graduated together, and they became close friends.

On the long Labor Day weekend, they decided to drive to San Francisco and celebrate the holiday there. They checked into a hotel. As soon as they were alone together, there was no doubt in either of their minds what they both wanted. They just simply read their desires in their faces.

They undressed and fell into bed without either having said a word to the other. They spent the entire weekend in the hotel room. It turned out that the other soldier was a virgin too, and they were both intent on making up for lost time. They were able to enjoy each other for over a year after that wonderful weekend, and then they were issued orders which separated them.

A short time earlier, Spenser had been called into the office of the base commander. He was told that he was being deployed to Afghanistan because he spoke Arabic, and his services would be vital as a translator. Martin never questioned his orders, but for some strange reason, he thought about his mother's Uncle Ibrahim.

He took a commercial flight to Northwest Florida Regional Airport, and from there he was to fly on a military transport to his ultimate destination. He was just settling into his seat, when a friendly accented voice said, "Hello, Martin. It's so nice to see you again."

He looked up into the icy black eyes of Uncle Ibrahim. Martin had an uneasy feeling, but he shook his uncle's hand, and said, "Nice to see you too. Quite a coincidence, isn't it?" Martin did not delude himself for one moment that this was a coincidence.

After they were seated and the plane lifted off on its flight to New York, Ibrahim started to talk to Spenser in Arabic. "I understand that you are going to Afghanistan as a translator." Spenser was shocked. How the hell did he know that?

"So?" he asked in English.

"Speak Arabic. You should practice," Ibrahim said in Arabic.

"I don't need practice," Martin retorted in English. He actually exaggerated his Midwestern accent.

"As you wish," his uncle replied in English.

"What's on your mind, Uncle," Martin tried sounding polite. He didn't feel like being polite after what his mother had revealed to him.

"This is your opportunity to serve Allah. I am sure there will be many things you will learn that would serve our cause well, should we be aware of them."

"I'm sure you are correct, Uncle. But what makes you think that I would do such a thing? More importantly, why should you trust me, and why should I trust you?"

"I trust you because you are a true son of Allah. Your father had no religion and your mother taught you hers. Your attendance at church at the Academy was mandatory. I know your heart wasn't in it."

"How the hell do you know so much about me?"

"We have been keeping you and your parents under surveillance since you were born." Suddenly Martin had a disquieting thought. Could his father's embolism not have been an embolism at all? He shuddered at the thought.

"I know that this is a big decision for you to make, but I will give you my card again, and I want you to think long and hard about where your loyalties lie." Ibrahim turned his back to his nephew, and they never spoke again until the end of the trip.

As they left the plane, Martin's Uncle said to him, "It would be wise for you to consider that we are aware of your hotel stays with that other Lieutenant." His uncle might just as well have hit him with a ten ton sack of concrete but Martin kept his composure. He did not answer, but walked quickly away from his uncle.

All Martin had with him was a carry-on bag. Even though he had no luggage, he literally ran to the baggage claim, where someone was to meet him. He immediately spotted an air force staff sergeant who was holding a placard with his name on it. He approached the sergeant, and the man saluted Martin smartly. They exchanged a few swift words, and Martin was led to a private parking area where the two men boarded a Jeep and the sergeant drove to Eglin Air Force Base. It appeared that Martin was to fly to Afghanistan in an air force transport.

Upon arrival in Afghanistan, Martin was escorted to his final destination by a good looking young sergeant. He saluted Martin and said, "I'm Sgt. Young, Lieutenant. We have about a two hour drive ahead of us. Is there something you need to do at this airport before we head out?"

"I wouldn't mind a good long pee, if that's alright with you."

"Of course. I should do the same before we leave."

Along the way, Sgt. Young engaged Martin in animated conversation about what life would be like for him in Afghanistan. By the end of the trip, Martin was calling Sgt. Young, Jim, and Jim was calling him Martin. But when other people were around they addressed each other formally.

Martin expected to arrive at a big compound, housing prisoners of war, whom he would interrogate. Instead, Jim drove them to a deserted village. They stopped in front of an old shack. "We're here," Jim said. The two men went inside. There was an army major sitting at a small desk, and a corporal was taking notes as the major dictated. The major smiled broadly when Martin came in. Martin saluted him, and he introduced himself as Major Jordan Carter. The two officers shook hands, and the major asked Jim and the corporal to leave them alone.

"I can see you are looking rather perplexed," Carter said. "Let me fill you in on things quickly. Interrogating these guys is useless. They won't tell us a thing. You can't crack religious fanatics. They want us to kill them so they can fly straight to paradise. If we try to use, shall we say, more persuasive means of interrogations, the outside world brands us as barbarians. They seem to forget all the terrorist attacks on America, Israel, and I don't know how many other countries.

The World Trade Center is like ancient history to these bleeding hearts. They fail to see that if we can break these scumbags by any means, we may well be saving hundreds of UN and American lives."

Carter paused and gazed at Martin. He was trying to read something in Martin's face, but Martin remained stoic.

"We have formulated a plan, but we need help, and you have the perfect profile to be the man we need," Carter continued.

"What is that, sir?"

"I'll try to digest it for you. For two or three months, we want you at the POW camp. You will conduct questioning in Arabic and try to gain the trust of the prisoners, if at all possible. During that time, you will make snide remarks about your superiors and their disrespect for Islam. Let them know that you are fed up with the non-believers. Then you will help two or three of them escape, and you will defect with them.

Our soldiers will carefully avoid firing anywhere we know you might be. You will try to capture one of our own. If you can't, we will arrange a capture for you. You will make those phony video tapes, showing how well taken care of your hostage is. They always hide the hostages and their captors in some remote spot. A courier picks up the film to be aired. We will be constantly observing you and we will follow the courier to their headquarters where, God willing, we'll capture or kill if need be, their big guns."

Martin did not say a word. He remained perfectly silent. Finally Carter asked, "Are you in? We can't force you."

Martin reached into his wallet and pulled out a card. "I can make it easier than you think," he said. "This is my uncle's card. All I need to do is call him after I have been at the interrogation camp for a few weeks. I'll tell him I'm planning on defecting, because I can't stand how the prisoners are being treated and the total disrespect for Islam. He'll help me infiltrate the enemy camp. He'll revel in it. He has been trying to enroll me in the Army of Allah for some time now."

Carter stood up and shook Martin's hand. "Good man," he said.

Part Four

Martin had outlived his usefulness in the Mideast. Both sides now knew that he was a mole. He was offered a discharge from the army or stateside reassignment. Had he not met Trevor, he would have stayed in the service. But at last he had found his soul mate, and he accepted his honorable discharge. He and Trevor were shipped home on an army transport which landed at Langley Air Force Base in Virginia.

From there, their next stop was Atlanta, Georgia where Trevor wanted to post the story of Martin's heroics with CNN but the government wouldn't let him. The operation was considered classified. Instead, Trevor asked for, and got a transfer to CNN headquarters in Chicago. He had no family, and since Martin feared for his mother's safety, they agreed to settle in Chicago.

Martin did not know his uncle's whereabouts. He had been placed on a dangerous persons' list, and flying into the US would be more difficult for him now. However, Martin knew that it would not be impossible, what with all the insurgent cells which existed throughout the world. As much as he feared his uncle, he feared telling his mother about his relationship with Trevor even more.

When they got off the plane at O'Hare, they went immediately to Baggage Claim. While they were waiting for their luggage, Martin grinned at Trevor. "You know what?" he asked. "We haven't been alone or unobserved since we met. Let's spend tonight in a hotel, and we'll go home tomorrow morning."

"I like how you think. Let's add a great stateside dinner to the scenario."

"You're on, buddy." Martin smiled. "I'll just call my mother and tell her that we have been delayed and will arrive tomorrow late in the morning."

When they checked into the hotel, Trevor noted that it was a good three hours until dinner time. They smiled at each other, undressed and jumped into the shower. They had incorrectly assumed that they would fuck each other in bed, but playing in the shower proved to be too arousing. Using soap as a lubricant, they finally unloaded in each other's guts. Afterwards, they clung to each other, unwilling to let go. Their energies were spent for the moment, so they climbed into bed and dozed for a couple of hours.

After dinner, they resumed making love. They started with a lusty game of sixty-nine. After both had cum, they kissed each other, and mixed their jism together in their dueling mouths. After a couple of hours, they were hard again and had no trouble fucking each other, this time using lubricant. They made love most of the night, and did not fall asleep until early in the morning.

While the two men were demonstrating their love for each other, Janina Spenser was awakened from a fitful sleep. She thought she heard a strange sound but she had been jumpy ever since her uncle's surprise visit so she dismissed it as being just her nerves. As a result, she was nearly wide awake, when someone bounded through her open bedroom door, and threw his body on top of her. His massive hands encircled her throat and began to choke her.

"You spawned a traitor," he yelled. "My brother is crying in Paradise because his grandson has spurned Allah. For this you will both die. I am disappointed. I thought your faggot son would be here tonight. No matter. I'll handle you one at a t...."

He never finished his sentence. Suddenly, blood gushed from his mouth and his neck and his massive frame slumped on Janina's tiny body. She was still having trouble breathing but she managed to push the body off her, and it rolled on the floor. She lay in bed sobbing and trying to catch her breath for almost an hour.

Finally, she calmed down enough to dial 911. Then she looked at her alarm clock with its luminous dial. It was five o'clock in the morning. She dialed Martin's cell phone, but unfortunately it was shut off and she didn't know where he was. She left him a message. "A terrible tragedy has occurred," she said. "Call me as soon as you can."

The paramedics treated her bruised neck, but she declined hospital attention. After she was cared for and the body was removed, the police took her statement.

"It was not I he was after," she explained. "I believe he was after my son, who was supposed to have come home last night, but will not be home until sometime this morning. The dead man is my uncle. He surprised us with a visit just before my son was deployed to the Middle East. He tried to get my son to agree to spy for the so called Army of Allah.

Naturally, my son refused. I have lived in fear ever since his visit so I have slept with a steak knife under my pillow all these months. When he started to choke me, I was able to reach under my pillow and thrust the knife into his neck. From the amount of blood he spewed out, I think I hit his jugular."

"Why do you think he was after your son?" the policeman asked.

"My son was on a secret mission for the army. I don't know what it was and I think it was classified."

The policeman was satisfied. "I'm going to leave a policewoman here with you until your son arrives," he said. "Why don't you change the bed sheets and try to get some rest. You're safe now."

When Trevor and Martin woke up, the sun was high in the sky. It was 10:30 AM. They showered together and played some more. They had until 1 PM to check out. By the time they were dressed and ready to vacate the room it was nearly noon and they decided to have brunch before heading to Trevor's home.

At brunch, Trevor said. "I love you, Martin, but there is one thing that really troubles me. I didn't want to ask, but now I must. Why did you kill Ahmed?"

"Ah, sweet love, did I not tell you before this? Ahmed was a spy for the other side. I knew that because I knew everyone who was aiding them. It was a pleasure to kill him. He had provided them with so much information to help them murder innocent people that he deserved to die."

Trevor gripped Martin's hand. "I should have known that you wouldn't kill an innocent man," he said.

Finally, when Martin reached into his pocket to pay the brunch bill, he retrieved his cell phone and turned it on. He saw that he had missed a call and he listened to the message. As he did, he turned white and the men rushed home in a cab.

They were greeted at the front door by a policewoman. "Thank God, you're here, Mr. Spenser," she said. "Your mother has been through quite a dreadful experience. Her uncle tried to kill her, but that spunky lady got him first."

"Where is she?" Martin's voice quivered as he looked around.

"I sent for a doctor and she gave your mother a sedative. Thankfully, she's finally asleep."

"Where's my uncle's body?"

"At the city morgue. I guess when they are through with him, he's all yours."

"Yes, I'll claim the body and give him an Islamic burial. It's more than he deserves."

"If you don't mind, I think I'll get back to the station now." She handed Martin a card. "If you need to go out of town, please call first. We may need to question you and your mother again." Her police car was in the driveway and she left abruptly.

Martin looked around at his surroundings. He was home and he was happy but apprehensive. His uncle had friends, and they would want revenge. He wasn't certain what to do. Just as a diversion he showed Trevor around his new home. Unfortunately, one of the first things they saw was the laundry room off the kitchen. The blood stained bed linens were lying in the hamper.

Martin did not care how costly the linens were. He picked them up, and stuffed them into the garbage can standing in the driveway just outside the mud room door. He didn't want his mother ever to see them again.

When he was done disposing of the bloody sheets, Martin took Trevor upstairs. There were only two bedrooms in the house, but fortunately each had its own bath. They looked in on Janina. She was sleeping peacefully. "She's as beautiful as I knew she would be," Trevor whispered in Martin's ear.

They went into Martin's room, and dropped their two small carryon bags on the floor. Trevor noted that the walk in closet was big enough for both of them, since neither had a lot of "stuff." In fact, Trevor had put all his belonging in three small cartons when they were in Atlanta, and he shipped them to Martin's home in Chicago. They should be arriving any moment.

There was only one standard size bed in the room. "What will your mother say to this?" Trevor asked Martin, pointing at the bed.

"It will be the moment of truth, sweetheart. I sure hope she accepts it, and likes you as much as I love you." They unpacked their small bags and put everything in a place. Then they went downstairs to wait for Janina to awaken.

"I'll make us some coffee," Martin said. While the coffee was brewing, he took some bread, butter and jam out of the refrigerator and popped the bread into the toaster. They were enjoying their little repast when Janina burst into the kitchen screaming with delight. She wrapped her arms around Martin and pulled his head down so that she could smother him with kisses.

She finally let go and looked at Trevor. "You must be Trevor," she smiled. "Martin has written so much about you, I feel like we are old friends." Trevor was surprised. He never saw Martin writing anything to anyone. He never even saw him use a computer. He could only wonder when he did it. Did he awaken before Trevor, and send messages from his phone? It was the only explanation.

"Sit down, Momma," Martin said softly. "I...we...have something to tell you. Trevor is coming to live with us permanently. He's a reporter for CNN, and most likely will travel more than I would like. As for me, I have landed a teaching position with The University of Chicago. I'll be teaching Arabic, as well as Islamic Studies."

"That's wonderful news." Janina was smiling broadly, and she went over to Trevor and kissed him on the cheek. "But we only have two bedrooms. Where will Trevor sleep, Martin?" Martin took a deep breath. "With me, Momma. We love each other and we are life partners."

Janina's face clouded over. "When my uncle tried to kill me, he called you a faggot, my son. I thought he was just trying to add to my misery, but I see it is true."

"Yes momma, it's true. If you only knew how much I love Trevor, you would understand."

Janina took her son's hand. "This is what I understand. When I am gone, you will not be alone. You will have a companion who will love you, share your life with you, look after you when you are sick, and be your lifetime crutch. For that I love Trevor already." Martin started to cry and Janina wrapped her arms around him once again.

"Now," she asked, "how long do we have to enjoy each other's company before you both have to go back to work."

"I start this coming Monday," Trevor said.

"And I start officially on the Tuesday after Labor Day in two weeks' time, but I have to go in for orientation on the Thursday and Friday before Labor Day. That gives us both the time to buy two automobiles."

"Martin, I rarely use my car. You might as well use it and then you only have to buy one new one." She smiled at the two men. "I want to cook all your favorite meals, but you'll have to tell me what your favorites are, Trevor."

"Not tonight," Martin interrupted. "Tonight we are celebrating at a five star restaurant. Now go upstairs and put on your best outfit, Momma. Trevor, our field jackets will have to be acceptable by the restaurant. We'll both need to shop for some clothes for work and for five star restaurants."

They all had a good laugh, and proceeded to get ready for an evening on the town. They might not have been so happy if they had seen the small black car parked discreetly up the street. Two men, sitting inside the car, were observing everything going on in the house, and everyone coming and going in and out of the house.

Part Five

Trevor and Martin started their jobs, and Janina resumed her role of being a stay at home mom. For a month it seemed that they could lead a normal, peaceful life. The black car still cruised the neighborhood and still parked discreetly a short distance from their house.

The men even began to venture out in the evenings, and they made some friends in the gay community. They had their favorite watering holes, but never stayed out late. They still feared for Janina's safety.

One day the inevitable happened. Trevor covered a disturbing story. SWAT teams had raided an apartment in downtown Chicago. The apartment had been under surveillance for months. The SWAT team confiscated enough explosives to blow up the whole city of Chicago. Unfortunately, the suspects, all known sympathizers of The Army of Allah, had somehow known about the raid, and were nowhere to be found. The sad news was that they were still at large.

Trevor immediately called Martin and told him to rush right home after work. He said that he would get home as soon as he could. Both men were certain that their little family was still a target for revenge.

As soon as Martin got Trevor's call, he locked his office door, and made a call to a secret number in Washington. Within a half hour, the number of men in the black car, which was cruising Martin's neighborhood, was increased to four.

Trevor and Martin maintained a happy attitude at home, and even made arrangements with Janina to take her out to dinner Saturday night for her birthday. The black car was now parked for the night, two doors down the street.

Trevor and Martin always closed their door when they retired for the night. They rigged the door so that a bell sounded if the door was opened without disengaging the apparatus from inside the bedroom.

Unknown to the men, Janina had replaced the steak knife under her pillow. She had even taken the time to sharpen the blade.

More than a week passed after the raid, without incident. Trevor and Martin had refrained from making love in all that time. Instead they lay awake listening for every sound in the house until sleep overcame them.

Finally, one night they relaxed a little bit and started to play. Trevor's hand enveloped Martin's massive tool and he began to stroke it. Martin reached over and began to masturbate Trevor. Lust took over and they twisted into a sixty-nine position. Both were close to orgasm when the bell clanged, indicating their door was being opened. They moved so quickly that they became a blur as each grabbed a pistol from underneath their pillows.

At least three men fell upon them. Two were quickly dispatched by blazing guns. The third stood back, shocked at what had occurred. He backed slowly toward the door, hoping to make an escape, and was rewarded for his efforts with a sharp knife in his back. Suddenly, lights were on throughout the house. Eight government agents were all over the place searching in every nook and cranny. Obviously, there had been more than one black surveillance car.

Trevor and Martin just managed to put boxers on when one of the agents came in the room. He grabbed Martin's hand and started pumping it.

"Captain Spenser," he said. "It's so good to see you again. And you too Mr. Lawrence," he said as an afterthought. It was Sgt. Jim Young, whom they had met in Afghanistan.

Trevor was confused. Jim called Martin, captain, when he knew he was a civilian now. That was odd enough, but last he had heard, Martin was a lieutenant when he was discharged. Jim hadn't saluted Martin, but then again, Martin was not in uniform.

"Good work once again, sir," Jim said. "We captured five more of them entering your house. I don't know if we got them all, but for sure, we've broken their back."

They had all forgotten Janina, who was cowering behind the bedroom door. She came out and looked around the bloody room. "Those bastards don't ever give me a chance to keep this house clean," she lamented. Everyone in the room was all keyed up, but they all broke out laughing.

"I know that it's very late," Jim said, "but could I ask you all to dress and come down to headquarters with me. We need to take your statements. I'll see to it that the bodies are removed."

Jim looked at Martin and winked. "Sorry for the interruption, sir." Martin turned red.

Trevor realized that somehow he had been kept in the dark about what had developed into a major army sting, and he was angry with Martin. On the other hand he wondered if he could get a story out of this after all, without endangering his family, that is.

They were escorted down town by the agents, so Trevor could not question Martin. Martin could sense the anger brewing in Trevor. He took Trevor's hand and looked in Trevor's eyes. His own eyes were pleading for time to explain. Trevor squeezed Martin's hand to let him know that he would be patient and understanding.

Much later that evening, when they were brought home, the three of them set about cleaning up the house and removing the evidence of the carnage that had occurred there. Sleep was out for the night. All three were operating on adrenalin. At last, Janina prepared breakfast, and she and Trevor looked at Martin waiting for a much needed explanation.

As they sipped their coffee, Martin finally began. "Everything was going according to plan regarding my transition into civilian life and then my mother's uncle tried to kill me and her. After the incident, I was contacted by a member of army intelligence. He was aware of my appointment to teach Arabic and Islamic studies at the university. He said that Chicago was one of the few schools in the nation that taught both. They were aware that The Army of Allah signed up many recruits from students in this program. The army offered to reinstate me as a captain, if I would agree to spy for them. I could keep an eye on my students, and hopefully recognize where their loyalties were. I accepted only because I believed we were all still in danger. I was certainly right about that. One of the men we killed tonight, and three of the men the army captured, were students of mine." Martin paused and glanced at the two dazed faces in front of him.

At last Trevor was able to talk. "How classified is this operation?" he asked. "Will any of it be made public?"

"Here's what you can write," Martin smiled at Trevor. He took a slip of paper out of his pocket and handed it to his partner.

Trevor read:

Although federal agents did not find any terrorists at the apartment, which they raided last week, they were able to identify everyone who came and went into the apartment. They raided a private home last night where three of the terrorists were killed and four more were captured. They were all members of a terrorist group called The Army of Allah.

The text was followed with a list giving the names, ages and citizenships of the dead and captured. There was no mention of any connection to the university or their teacher.

Trevor smiled at Martin and he pulled his telephone out of his pocket. He went into the living room and called in the story while Janina stared long and hard at her son. "We will always be in danger, won't we?" she asked.

"Yes, Momma, unfortunately we will always be on the enemy list of The Army of Allah. At least this way I can continue to do my part to thwart them, and to fight them. I'm so sorry."

"Don't be sorry," Janina said kindly. "I'm the one who set the stage when I ran away with your father. If this is the price we must pay for freedom, so be it."

Trevor returned with a grin on his face. "Thanks, Babe," he said, "Now let's talk. How long are you going to lead a double life?"

"Until I feel safe for all of us, no matter how many years it takes. Hey, look at it this way. The university is paying me and the army is paying me. I am earning two salaries and two pensions. We'll be able to retire in grand style in some tropical paradise."

"If we are lucky enough to survive. Hey kiddo, I told my boss I was up all night covering the story, and I wouldn't be in to work today."

"I'll call in sick also," Martin announced.

"I think I'll go to the mall after I clean up the kitchen," Janina said.

As soon as they heard her leave the house, Trevor and Martin went upstairs. They needed desperately to make love after being so rudely interrupted this past evening. They undressed rapidly with the intention of taking a shower and maybe fucking in the shower. They had been up all night, and had stayed awake for many nights before that listening for danger.

Suddenly neither of them could keep their eyes open. They fell naked on their bed and hunkered close. They grabbed each other's cocks and fell fast asleep. Their shower and their love making would have to wait until they woke up several hours later.

They were safe, at least for the moment. A black car with two passengers was parked serenely in front of the house. They could sleep tranquilly, and recover their strength.

The End

Here is a sample from another story you may enjoy:

HANK BROOKS

Lustful
DESIRES
Gay Romance

My name is Cory Henderson. I am nineteen years young, and I am gay. Nobody knows that about me, except me. It doesn't really matter. The only sex I have is with myself. I am still a virgin.

Unlike most gay men, I am heavily into sports. I am a gymnast, which is what stereotypically one would expect a gay man (into sports) to be. I am on my college's gymnastic team. I am good, but not good enough to have Olympic aspirations. I suspect that at least one other member of my team is gay, but I am not entirely sure, and I am not about to come onto him. If he has any suspicions about me, I would imagine he feels the same way, and wouldn't dare to out himself to me. Anyhow, I have no sexual desires for him.

I am built like a typical gymnast. I am only five feet, eight inches tall, but my muscles have muscles. I am aware of the admiring glances of my fellow students, both male and female. Unfortunately, only my teammates have seen my cock, and only in the shower, and only in its flaccid state. It's a five-inch, cut beauty. It has some heft as well, and reaches about seven inches when I whack off.

So far I have had no problem curbing my sexual appetite, or living with my secret. There is only one area of my life that is giving me trouble. Late last August, when I met my roommate for the first time, I was consumed with lust. Ray Jensen is an athlete also, and he plays football with our college team. He is six feet, two inches tall. His skin color is a light mocha. His body is hairy, whereas I am almost hairless. I know that he is nearly as muscular as I am, but he weighs two hundred fifty pounds. His muscles are somewhat hidden by some flab.

It doesn't matter to me. The first time I saw him naked, I gasped out loud, and Ray laughed. He is uncut and his monstrous black cock, when flaccid, is as big as mine is, when erect. It is also twice as fat around. I saw it hard the first morning we roomed together, and I believe it was as big as a baseball bat. Perhaps I exaggerate, but it seemed that way to me.

Sometime during the first week of the semester, I came back to our room very late in the evening. The gym team had really been put through the ropes that afternoon. Ray was sound asleep, lying naked in his bed. His cover sheet was pushed down to the foot of his bed. He was flat on his back, and his monster was at full mast. I found out later that the football team had been put through an equally rigorous practice session. Ray had come home just a few minutes before me, and collapsed into bed.

He smelled fresh, and I realized his team must have showered before going home, just as mine had. I closed and locked our door and stood frozen, staring at him. I wanted desperately to stroke his cock with my tongue. I didn't believe I could even get his cockhead into my mouth. His luscious, dark purple head had fully unsheathed itself from his black foreskin, and it was facing the ceiling.

I approached his bed, and I swear I began to bend down toward his inviting rod. He smelled so good I almost swooned. Suddenly Ray groaned in his sleep, jolting me back to reality. I couldn't stand to look at his cock, so I took his cover sheet and draped it across his body. It didn't do much to hide the object of my lust. There was a fair sized pyramid outlined in the sheet.

As soon as he was covered, Ray mumbled, "Thanks, buddy."

Good God. He was awake. I shuddered at the thought of what might have happened if I had given into my lustful desires. I might be telling you this story from beyond the grave.

After that I did everything in my power to avoid seeing Ray undressed, but that was nearly impossible. We both slept naked, and more often than not, we ran into each other when we were showering in the morning.

One time, Ray asked me to wash his back. I needed to defuse my lust, so I laughed and said, "Sure, you want me to do your back so you can grab my cock." I laughed as hard as I could, and ran out of the shower.

While we were drying ourselves, Ray started to laugh also. "Sorry Buddy," he said, "I was serious back there, and for your information, I had no ulterior motive. Don't be so sensitive. I have no desire to get into your pants."

I wanted to say, "You can get into my pants any day of the week, big guy," but instead I said, "I'm sorry too. I guess I am too sensitive."

From that day on, I noted a subtle change in Ray. He still slept naked, but he was careful to remove his boxers after he got into bed, and he never seemed to shower at the same time that I did any more. Certainly I was glad about that, but the idea of his avoiding me while in the nude, disturbed me somehow.

Just before winter break, we were both lying in bed, talking about how much we were looking forward to going home. Both of us lived too far away to have gone home for the short Thanksgiving holiday. We had each packed a small suitcase and were going to share a cab to the bus depot immediately after our last class the next day. I don't remember it happening, but I fell asleep in the middle of our conversation. I usually pee before I go to bed, but I didn't that night. As a result I woke up about 2 AM.

I was about to step out of bed, and grab my robe to go to the bathroom, when I heard strange grunting noises coming from Ray's bed. I knew that sound well. Ray was whacking off. As badly as I needed to pee, I decided to wait until he was finished. I had no idea if he would be embarrassed or not if I caught him. I wondered how I would feel if he caught me going at it. I didn't get an answer from me.

I was trying desperately to get a peek at what was going on. There was enough moonlight coming into the room, that at the very least, shadows were discernible. I turned my head very slightly, and my efforts were rewarded. I distinctly saw a tube of lube on the bed stand between our two beds. Beyond that, Ray had his hand wrapped around his cock, and was stroking slowly. At least three inches of his cock protruded above his extra huge palm. Every so often Ray stopped stroking. After a short rest, he resumed. I realized that he was doing all he could to prolong his orgasm. That was well and good, but if I didn't pee soon, I was going to wet my bed.

Finally, I could bear it no longer. I pretended I couldn't see anything. I got out of bed, grabbed my robe and ran out of the room. When I got back, Ray was under his cover sheet and lying on his side. I didn't know if he had finished or if he had given up because of my intrusion. My question was answered about a half hour later.

After I peed, I was unable to fall asleep again. Ray must have thought otherwise. I heard him throw off his covers. I peeked at him through a barely opened single eye. He turned on his back, and continued where he left off when I got out of bed. I guess he wasn't greased enough, because he reached over for the tube of lube, and replenished the grease on his palm.

I continued to play possum. Eventually I heard Ray's stifled scream. I also thought I heard him mutter someone's name. I peeked and saw his fist in his mouth. I'd give anything to know whose name he called out. I wanted to know what lucky girl was the object of his masturbation fantasies.

After his jerking body calmed down, he reached under his pillow and took out some facial tissues. He cleaned himself as best he could. Finally, he got out of bed and threw his tissues in our trash can. He put the tube of lube into one of his dresser drawers. Grabbing his bathrobe, he left the room for a few minutes.

I don't know what devil possessed me while Ray was out of the room, but I decided to make him uncomfortable. When he came back, I sat up in bed and asked, "Are you OK, Ray?"

"You're awake?" he gasped.

"Yeah, I've been up since about 2 AM. I couldn't go back to sleep. What time is it now?"

"It's about four."

"Shit," I said, "get back in bed. Maybe we can get a couple more hours of sleep." I rolled over smiling, leaving him to wonder if I had caught him in the act of pleasuring himself. I sort of hoped he would ask, but he didn't. I rolled over and smiled. I actually fell asleep, and the next thing I knew it was 6:30 AM.

When I got up, Ray got up also. For the first time in a long time, we showered at the same time. For some reason, I wasn't afraid to stare at him, and I didn't care if he noticed or not.

After our last class, we returned to our room and picked up our suitcases. The cab we had hired was waiting outside. At the bus depot, we jumped out of the cab, waved at each other and went our separate ways.

The minute I turned my back on Ray, I missed him terribly. I hallucinated that we each dropped our suitcase, turned around, and started to run toward each other in slow motion. We never connected. We just kept running and running. The joy of going home for Christmas suddenly gave way to a deep despair.

If you enjoyed this sample then look for **Lustful Desires**.

Also by this Author

Silver Spoon

Ordinary Guy

South Beach Rhapsody

Sensual Bet Rendezvous

Accidentally-in-Love

Lost Emotion

A Commuter's Obsession

Forgiven

Shower Mate

Year-Ender Surprise

The Underdog

Service with Love

The Second Time Around

A Comfortable Sorrow

Personal Choice

Doubtful Heart

As You Are

40th Pleasure

The Love Act

Harry's Trial

About the Author

He was born many years ago in the small town of Brooklyn, NY. His childhood was not a happy one. He was overweight and terrible at all the street games the other kids played. By the time he got to Brooklyn College, he was all slimmed down and smart enough to avoid athletics.

Married at 21, the union produced three fantastic overachievers who subsequently produced five sons between them. He discovered he was gay at a later part of his life. He now lives with his fantastic partner, Leo, in Coconut Creek, Florida.

He has been writing gay stories for a good number of years now and has gained the support of a lot of fans from his written stories. He is also the writer of many more books published by this name, Hank Brooks on Amazon.

From the Author

Check my page on Amazon for Updates and interesting info.

Author Central - http://www.amazon.com/Hank-Brooks/e/B00CKI1Y1Y

If you enjoyed any of my books then please share the love and click like on my books in Amazon.

If you write me a review and send me an email I will send you a free book, or many. (Just know that these emails are filtered by my publisher.)

Good news is always welcome.

One Last Thing, For Kindle Readers...

When you turn the page, Kindle will give you the opportunity to rate this book and share your thoughts on Facebook and Twitter. If you enjoyed my writings, would you please take a few seconds to let your friends know about it? Because... when they enjoy they will be grateful to you and so will I.

Thank You!

Hank Brooks
hank_brooks@awesomeauthors.org